CONFESSIONS
OF a SPONGE

Stephen Hillenburg

Based on the TV series *SpongeBob SquarePants*®
created by Stephen Hillenburg as seen on Nickelodeon®

SIMON SPOTLIGHT
An imprint of Simon & Schuster Children's Publishing Division
1230 Avenue of the Americas, New York, New York 10020
© 2006 Viacom International Inc. All rights reserved. NICKELODEON, *SpongeBob SquarePants*, and all related titles, logos, and characters are registered trademarks of Viacom International Inc. Created by Stephen Hillenburg.
All rights reserved, including the right of reproduction in whole or in part in any form.
SIMON SPOTLIGHT and colophon are registered trademarks of Simon & Schuster, Inc.
Manufactured in the United States of America
First Edition
10 9 8 7 6 5 4 3 2 1
ISBN-13: 978-1-4169-1570-6
ISBN-10: 1-4169-1570-2

CONFESSIONS
OF a SPONGE

BY SaraH WiLLSON

Simon Spotlight/Nickelodeon
New York   London   Toronto   Sydney

Hello. We're here in Bikini Bottom to interview a certain important sponge.

His name: SpongeBob SquarePants.

Our mission: To find out the untold story, by recording his confessions, and by interviewing those who know him best. What lies beneath that porous yellow exterior? What makes this sponge different from the rest? That's what we have come to find out.

Shh! Here he comes now.

Sir! Sir! May we have a moment of your time?

Sure! I'm ready to tell you anything you want to know about me! First of all I confess that I live right here in Bikini Bottom. For those of you who don't know how to get to Bikini Bottom, you need to find the Pacific Ocean, and then go *under* it. rodger that.

Why do you live in a pineapple? What were you like as a baby?

I live in a pineapple because it's the perfect size for me and my pet snail, Gary. Also it's right next to the houses of my two best friends, Patrick and Squidward.

I don't remember too much about being a baby. For that, you'd better interview my family. They'll tell you everything you need to know!

Mr. Squarepants

We knew our son was special from the day he was born! The nurses at the maternity ward told us they'd never, ever, heard a baby laugh quite like him! They kept shaking their heads and muttering that we were going to have quite a handful. It turns out they were right!

As a baby, SpongeBob loved having his hands full of stuff. Look where it got him too! Today he's at the top of his profession when it comes to handling all the ingredients for a Krabby Patty!

MRS. SQUAREPANTS

I remember SpongeBob's first tricycle! The day we took him to choose his new trike, the salesman let him test-drive it in the toy aisle. SpongeBob was so cute! How was he supposed to know there was breakable merchandise in the next aisle?

He loved that little red trike, even though he never quite mastered the art of riding it. We've replanted all the bushes he knocked down along the driveway. No *wonder* SpongeBob loves boating school so much!

I also remember the first time he went jellyfishing with his father. Little SpongeBob caught a big one! Of course the jellyfish insisted on being let go, and SpongeBob's daddy was in bed for a week with stings.

My mother says I showed signs of future greatness!

She just had to look for them under a microscope.

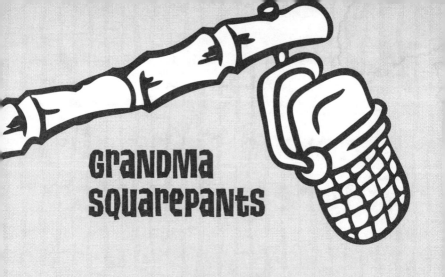

GRANDMA SQUAREPANTS

My grandson, SpongeBob, always was a dear boy. I used to knit him warm woolly sweaters.

There was love in every stitch.

He still visits me regularly. He never forgets to wipe his feet on the mat. What more could a grandmother wish for in a grandson? And he always remembers my birthday. Why, he took me out to lunch for my birthday last year! We went to a lovely little place called the Krusty Krab. I ordered a Krabby Patty, and it was delicious! It turns out that's where SpongeBob works! It was my birthday, so his nice boss gave us a .0001 percent discount on the bill, and free refills on water!

I give my family all the credit for the success that I have achieved today. My family has taught me so many things. My mom taught me to eat my vegetables. I have a seaweed salad every day—for roughage! And my dad taught me to keep a jar of sea-nut butter on hand for unexpected guests—you never know when someone might pop in for a visit!

And I always wear clean, freshly pressed underwear—because, as my grandmother used to point out, what if I got into a fender-bender and had to go to the doctor with wrinkled underwear? what if

Gary

My pet snail, Gary, is the best companion a sponge could have. Aren't you, Gary?

Meow!

He keeps the house spick-and-span, except for the occasional trail of snail slime. There are a couple of things Gary says he wants to confess. First of all he hates being left alone. Hey, Gar, remember the time I went away for the weekend? You chewed up the couch, remember? He loves to go for walks around the block, which can take several hours.

Gary also wants to confess how much he loves to play fetch with me. Sometimes I can read the entire newspaper before he comes back. Right, Gar-bear?

Meow.

Patrick Star

Hi. I'm Patrick Star. SpongeBob and I are best friends. We do all kinds of stuff together.

OUR FAVORITE THING TO DO IS GO JELLYFISHING. WE ALSO LIKE TO PLAY WITH SQUIDWARD. HE DOESN'T TAKE TIME TO HAVE FUN, SO WE TRY TO HELP HIM WHENEVER WE CAN. I KNOW HE REALLY APPRECIATES IT WHEN WE INCLUDE HIM.

WHAT ELSE? OH! I LIVE UNDER A ROCK. I ONCE GOT AN AWARD FOR DOING NOTHING LONGER THAN ANYONE ELSE. I WAS SO PROUD. Emily May came in at a close 2nd.

YOU WANT ME TO TELL YOU SOMETHING ABOUT SPONGEBOB?
OKAY, LET ME THINK.
OH, YEAH! THIS ONE TIME?
SPONGEBOB AND ME?
WE . . . UM . . . UH . . .
I FORGET. BUT IT WAS AWESOME.
BY THE WAY, WHAT DOES "CONFESS" MEAN?

SQUIDWARD TENTACLES

You want my confessions about SpongeBob? Puh–leeze. Why are you guys doing a story about *him*, anyway? You should be doing a story about me! *I'm* the one who plays the clarinet!

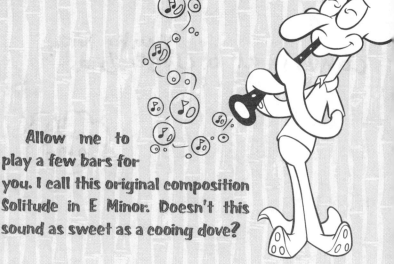

Allow me to play a few bars for you. I call this original composition Solitude in E Minor. Doesn't this sound as sweet as a cooing dove?

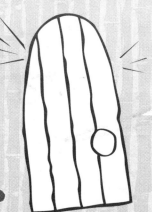

It's the dentist! Open up! I heard someone screaming in pain from a toothache! What?

Not only do I have the "pleasure" of living next to SpongeBob, I have to *work* with him too! He torments me night and day! And so does his friend Patrick! Can you believe they actually think I *like* to play with them? The last time they dragged me out jellyfishing I ended up in the hospital.

get out my li

SANDY CHEEKS

loser

SpongeBob is my buddy. We have tons of fun together. In fact having a great time is what I like to do best! You want to know what SpongeBob and I do for fun in Bikini Bottom? Well, I'll make you a list faster 'n a barefoot jackrabbit on a greasy griddle on a dog day in August!

Things I like to do with the square yellow dude:

karate
sippin' tea in my treedome
talkin' about Texas
hangin' out at Goo Lagoon
surfin'

(see pg. 40)

pearl

Am I on camera? Like, right now? How do I look? This is so coral I can't believe it. I have to call Jen!

I know SpongeBob because he works at my dad's restaurant. I don't like to hang out at the Krusty Krab too much. It's bad for my complexion. Once I tried to spruce up the place, but my dad, like, hated spending money so it didn't work out. I like going to the mall, cheerleading, and hanging out with my friends. I don't see SpongeBob that much, but he *did* take me to my prom. I thought he was going to completely, like, embarrass me, but in the end we had a beachy time (before we got kicked out).

← underpants

MRS. PUFF

at least he's <u>trying</u> to get his license.

SpongeBob has been my student for a very long time. I'll never forget the day that my troubles began. It was the day I met him. I had just made a pledge that I will regret for as long as I live.

With the opening of my new boating school, I pledge that as long as a student is willing to learn, I shall never give up!

RULES of the ROAD

Sometimes you jus have to know when t give up.

24

SpongeBob is a very dedicated student, I admit. Last week he stayed after school every day. He clapped the erasers, cleaned my classroom, polished the Good Noodle Stars board, and knitted seat covers for every chair in the classroom.

Just today he appointed himself Chief of Chewing-Gum Patrol. He removed chewed gum from every surface in the classroom. So while I admit that he is a very eager student, I think I need to confess that HE HAS FAILED HIS BOATING TEST THIRTY-EIGHT TIMES!! I can't be *that* bad a teacher, can I?

Don't answer that!

Where do you work, SpongeBob?

Behold! My fry-cook station at the Krusty Krab! This is my training manual. I memorized every word of it, right down to the punctuation! See what it says here on page 723? P-O-O-P. That stands for "People Order Our Patties!"

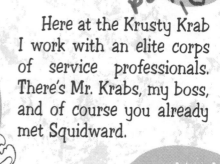

you're laughing because it says poop! ♥ U

Here at the Krusty Krab I work with an elite corps of service professionals. There's Mr. Krabs, my boss, and of course you already met Squidward.

I have dreamed of being a fry cook my whole life. And now I consider myself part of a dream team. Our mission: To make the best darn Krabby Patties in the world, and to bring honor and glory to the Krusty Krab! Sorry, have to run. A tour bus full of hungry customers just pulled up!

MR. KRABS

SpongeBob is a good lad. He works hard. And the nice thing is, I never need to give him a raise! He's happy just to get the Employee-of-the-Month award! He's gotten the award many months in a row. But we need to do a bit of belt-tightening around here.

SpongeBob, me boy! Remember that .0001 percent discount I gave ye when yer grandmother came in? I was just kidding! I'm afraid I need to take that outta yer next paycheck, lad. And no more free refills on water! Let's put an eyedropper at the condiment station to dispense the ketchup. The customers are using too much of the stuff!

I still don't understand why you guys are interested in *him*. Here's a list of things *I* want to talk about!

Things that make me happy:

clarinet recitals
modern dance
soufflé recipes
bubble baths
tentacle manicures
dining at five-star restaurants

What other careers interest you, SpongeBo

Plankton is always trying to get me to work at Chum Bucket, but my place is here at the Krusty Kra

> Unless, of course, I come up with an evil plan to control his brain and get him to come work for me! Once I get the formula for Krabby Patties I shall be one step closer to World Domination! Mwah-ha-ha!!!

I've often thought I might make a great taxi driver. Maybe some day, if I pass my boating exam, that might be a good second job for me.

I once had a job as a stand-up comedian. Want to hear one of my jokes?

Okay . . . let's talk about tomatoes. What's up with them, anyway? I mean, are they fruits, or vegetables? And have you ever thought about ketchup? I mean, what is it, a fruit or a vegetable puree? Uh, is this microphone working? This is the part where you're supposed to laugh.

What are your thoughts on parenthood, SpongeBob?

I think parenthood is a *great* idea! If there were no parents, none of us would be here! I was a parent once . . . to a wee scallop. Patrick and I adopted it and nurtured it along until it was ready to leave the nest. And once, our friends Em & Gina adopted a chinese babo from China and raised it in VT.

Sniff! It was one of the hardest, most rewarding experiences of my life! They grow up so fast.

What are you afraid of, SpongeBob?

I'm afraid of hardly anything . . .

. . . except, of course . . .

giant clams,
icy-cold stethoscopes at the doctor's office,
bullies,
menacing sea worms,
sea bears,
the hash-slinging slasher,
falling on my butt, —→ word
and pretty much anything to do with Halloween.

← his butt

Tell us about your travels, SpongeBob.

I haven't traveled to that many places because I don't have my boating license yet. Maybe the thirty-ninth time will be the charm! By this time next semester I'd like to be hittin' the road a lot, seein' the sights. In the meantime one of my *favorite* places to walk to is Jellyfish Fields. That's where my friends and I go to catch jellyfish, but of course we always let the jellyfish go.

Sometimes Patrick and I go camping, but we're a little scared of sea bears so we don't go very often.

And you know what? There's no place I would rather be than right here in Bikini Bottom. There's no place like home, don't you think? I mean, if you *really* want to travel, all it takes is your . . .

imagination!

SpongeBob's rules to live by:

BE TRUE TO YOUR FRIENDS!

☑ check

Always be there for your friends,
and they will be there for you.

LAUGH A LOT!

check!

DARE TO DREAM ✓

I dream of the day I finally get my driver's license.

The thirty-ninth road test—that's what I dream about. I wake up screaming.

issues.

I like to dream that I'm playing the clarinet in front of a huge audience.

WHAT DO I DREAM ABOUT? RIDING THE MECHANICAL HORSEY OUTSIDE THE GROCERY STORE. ditto

In my dreams I'm the world champion of everything! Josh?
including bowling, friendship,
bar hopping, bingo, and being a weiner

I dream about the day I finally have the Krabby Patty recipe in my hands!!!

See? Everyone has a dream!

WORK HARD – eh?

I feel like when I'm working hard, I'm hardly working! *false*.

DEVELOP YOUR OWN PERSONAL STYLE ✓

If you're like me, you'll find a look that works and stick with it! 'Course, I don't mind changing my look when the mood strikes me!

And above all . . .

43

go away

44

Thank you, Mr. SquarePants. Your story is truly an inspiring one, but I just found out that I was supposed to interview a different guy over in *Tank*ini Bottom.

ALL RIGHT, CREW! PACK IT IN. WE HAVE THE WRONG SPONGE!

So I guess you're not important after all. Well, you'll always be important to me, SpongeBob.
Em— I have a confession— You're important to me and I love you. I have the most F-U-N with you. Thanks pal, Gina
i'm touching your butt
1
2
3
4 nipples.